Published by B & F Publishing, Spokane, Washington

Developed in Post Falls, Idaho by Crown Media and Printing, Inc.
www.crownmediacorp.com

ISBN# 978-1-4507-3350-2

Cougar Cub Tales

Lost and Alone

Written and Illustrated by
Sharon Cramer

Dedicated to Vonnie

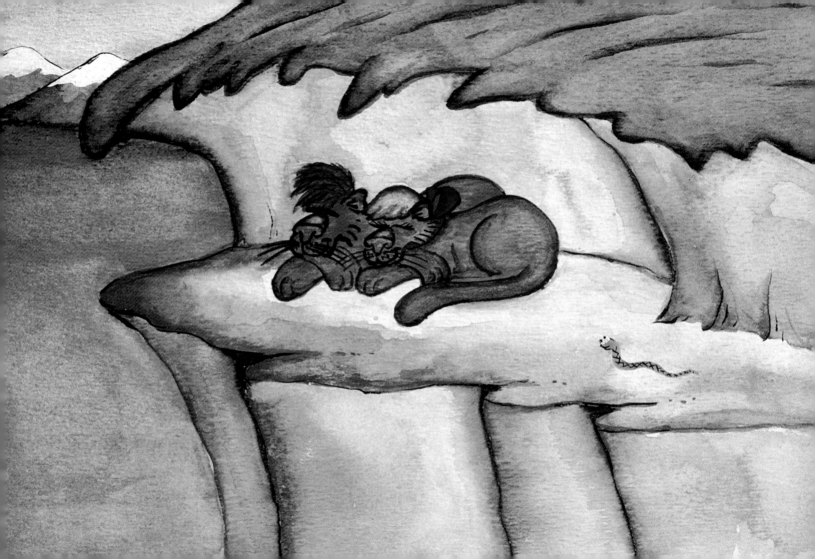

The cougar cub kittens were sister and brother.

They lived in their den, just one and the other,

For in a terrible snow... long ago...

They had lost their dear mother.

They played hide and seek,

Leapfrog and tag,

Catch-a-cat-can

And ziggety-zag.

They scampered and scompered

This way and the other,

And frequently trompered

Upon one another.

Together the cougar cubs happily raced.

For lizards and rabbits they hunted and chased.

They pounced, bounced and flounced

After wild wooly bears,

Till tired they dragged fuzzy tails without cares.

Then one day for some reason

Neither are sure,

They growled and they hissed

And they spat cougar Grrrrrrs!

Till neither would speak,

Not him and not her,

And separate they went

With scarcely a purrrrr...

"Oh how big the world is...

I never realized!"

The girl cougar noticed

With big widened eyes.

"I never saw such a big forest

As this...

It never did seem quite so scary

With sis..."

Till finally each cougar paused in their paws,

And lonely recalled their own cougar flaws,

And realized the saddest moment that day

Was when each the other had wandered away...

And as the sun set and darkness did fall,

Each cougar cub felt so lonely and small,

And not just because night had darkenly come,

But because they were separate,

Not together... at home...

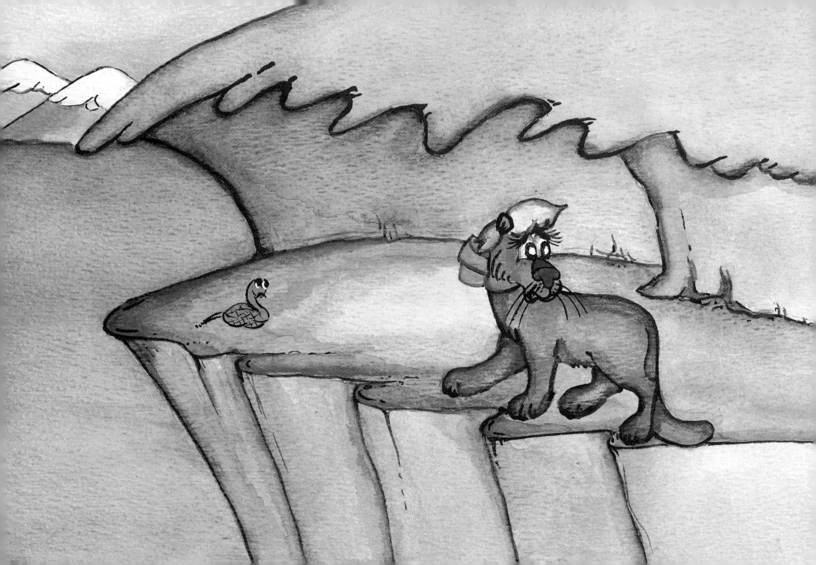

Then each cub abounding returned to the den,

But girl cougar made it more quickly than him.

And seeing that brother was nowhere around,

Set out determined that he should be found...

And he likewise found the den

Empty and cold,

And just as his sister did...

Set out abold...

October did turn

And what once was aglow,

Did suddenly frost,

And then blow... and then snow!

Till where cougar cubs

Had once hunted for lizard,

There blew down upon them

An icy cold blizzard!

But somehow a cougar cub angel was watching.

She led the cubs path to a rocky outcropping.

And even though frizzen and shivren in snow,

The cubs hugged each other,

Their hearts all aglow,

For nothing is warmer than cub-love you know!

Beneath the outcropping they huddled together,

And bravely as lions they weathered the weather.

And when the storm lifted and dawn slowly brightened,

They peered out in awe at their world all awhitened!

Then springing forth

Burst through the dander-deep snow,

And scampered and scompered together as though

They had never been parted, away from their den.

And sure as there's angels...

Never would be again.

The End

Sharon Jean Cramer was born in Jamestown, New York in 1960. She has lived throughout the United States, finally settling in the Pacific Northwest. She went to Idaho State University and then Gonzaga University. She is married and has three sons of her own. She and the cougar cubs currently reside, happily, in Spokane, Washington.

Other books by Sharon Cramer:
• Cougar Cub Tales: I'm Just Like You
• Cougar Cub Tales: The Sneezy Wheezy Day

Child labor was not used in the production of this book.
B & F Publishing and Crown Media & Printing, Inc print the Cougar Cub Tales in an ISO 9001 certified workplace that has been approved by the BSCI (Business Social Compliance Initiative)